The Taking of Sara

I0778976

KENNETH WALTER

Copyright 2025 by Kenneth Walter

ISBN: 978-1-966615-21-7 (Paperback)

All rights reserved. This book or any portion thereof may not be reproduced or used in any manner whatsoever without the express written permission of the publisher except for the use of brief quotation in a book review.

CONTENTS

CHAPTER 1

The nations of earth (Terra) are living in harmony and Terra has been accepted into the Galactic Federation of Worlds (GFW). It is now 20 years after Joe and the aliens made this possible. The GFW craft are seen patrolling the sky over the whole earth. There is occasional fighting between them and other malevolent aliens who want to do us harm.

Hickory is still a small town although several new businesses have started, and the population has grown. The crime rate is very low. Some domestic crimes are still committed, most of it is from out-of-town troublemakers. The pillory is still in front of City Hall but is seldom used. It is more of a monument and deterrence for crime than an actual punishment device.

Gas stations and electric charging stations have gone out of business because now cars run on their own power cells. New ones are being developed that can fly, but the problem of three-dimensional traffic control has not been solved. Some new houses are being built that are not connected to an electric power grid. They are using the same power cell technology used in the cars. A new medical facility, Hickory Healing Hospital (HHH), has been constructed where all manner of illnesses, including cancer, chronic and autoimmune diseases, are now cured by use of medbeds, which were made possible by use of alien technology. Far infrared, various photon and sound frequencies as well as other techniques, such as genetic modifications, are being utilized.

Jet airplanes are no longer used. People now fly in aircraft that do not use fuel. These new advances were made possible by use of alien technology.

Joe is now Quality Control Manager at the furniture factory. He manages 5 employees who have responsibility over various stages of furniture manufacturing from purchasing of raw materials to the final product.

Joe and Ann are still living in her mother's house that she inherited when her mother died several years ago. They now have two children; Dan and Sara. Dan is eighteen and Sara is fifteen years old. They all regularly attend church service. Ann and Sara sing in the choir and Joe is a deacon who helps serve communion with assistance from his son Dan.

Dan and Sara have adjoining bedrooms upstairs. Joe and Ann have the master bedroom on the first floor.

Dan and Sara are both in high school. Dan is a senior who likes astronomy and computer science. He has an analytical mind and likes to find out how things work. He wants to study alien technology and become a space craft pilot.

Sara is a high school freshman who likes physiology and anatomy. She has a friendly, outgoing personality and likes flowers. She wants to go to medical school and become a doctor.

CHAPTER 2

THE TAKING

One night Dan heard loud humming and clicking sounds from Sara's room. He quickly pulled on his pants and went to investigate. There was a bright blue light coming in through her window. Sara was not in her bed. He checked and it was still warm where she had been sleeping. When he went to look out of the window the blue light was fading away and a vibrating humming sound was coming from above. He looked up and saw a large discoidal craft that immediately disappeared from sight. He ran downstairs and burst into his parent's bedroom, waking them instantly. When he told them what had happened, they all ran upstairs to her room. It was empty as Dan had said. There was a lingering faint odor that smelled like burnt sulfur. Joe realized immediately that she had been abducted by aliens. They were all terrified about what had happened. Joe knew that they would need help to get her safely back and explained this to Ann and Dan.

When they went back downstairs, Joe's alien acquaintance #5, his contact from the previous work to enable Terra to be a member of the GFW, was waiting in the front room. He said, "I sensed Sara's strong emotion of fright and came as soon as I could but missed her abduction. What can you tell me about this?"

Dan told him about the sounds, blue light and the craft he saw. Joe added that the room had a faint odor of burning sulfur.

#5 said, "I have an idea who the abductors are but will need to verify it with my supervisor and get back to you. We must act very quickly, or you may never get her back. Just wait here for me to return. I will get back to you as soon as I can."

Ann collapsed in a chair and began crying. Joe went over to her and tried to comfort her with assurance that #5 would return with a plan to get her back. Dan began pacing back and forth, cursing the ones that took her. Joe told him to calm down and that cursing them would do no good. He finally sat down by his mother, and they sobbed together in each other's arms. Joe offered a prayer for her safety and return.

The doorbell rang and Joe went to answer it. It was Bob, the next-door neighbor. He said, "Did you notice a bright blue light outside last night?"

Joe answered, "I did not notice the light, but Dan did. Our daughter Sara was abducted by aliens last night. The light was from their space craft."

Bob said, "OH NO, that is terrible. I thought that they were good for us."

Joe said, "They are very different from the ones that helped us. These are very bad. Like people, some are good and some are bad."

Bob asked if there was anything that he could do to help. Joe told him that one of the friendly aliens were already working with the GFW on a plan to get her back and that there was nothing he could do for now.

Bob turned to leave but stopped and faced Joe. "Be sure to let me know if there is anything I can do to help." Joe thanked him and said that he would do that.

A short time later, #5 appeared in front of them. "My suspicions were correct. I know who took her. They are an evil, violent, reptilian race called the Draco. They are very powerful, and it will be difficult to get her back even when we find out where they have taken her. My supervisor is meeting with the GFW council to form a recovery plan for your daughter. I will let you know when we have determined the best course of action."

Joe insisted that he be included in the plan. #5 said, "It would be too dangerous for you. Ann may end up losing you as well as Sara." After saying this, he disappeared.

After a few hours, he reappeared and said, "The Draco have a cloaking device on their craft that make them invisible, but it leaves a disturbance in the atmosphere that we can detect. They have taken her to their underground base in Antarctica. We had them eliminated from Terra once, but they have managed to slip back into this abandoned Antarctica base. We could go after them with force, but they may anticipate our attempt and take her and any others they have abducted to another location before we can act. My supervisor's conversation with the GFW council went well and they have agreed to help us. The Antarctic base was constructed by the Orion Collective. We can get a good layout of this base from them. When we have that information, we can formulate a plan to get Sara back. I will get back to you as soon as I can to update you on our progress."

#5 returned in about one hour and said, "The Ashtar Galactic Command (AGC) have agreed to work with the GFW. They were previously associated with the Alpha-Draconians, but broke away from them due to a difference of opinion on how Terra humans should be treated. It may be possible for them to send a delegation to the Draco in Antarctica and negotiate a release of any humans that they have abducted. These negotiations will take some time so you need to pray that Sara is being used in a way that she will not be harmed. I will get back to you as soon as possible."

CHAPTER 3

SARA

Sara slowly regained consciousness and opened her eyes but found that she could not move. The last thing she remembered was being asleep in her bed when she was awakened by the feeling that someone was in her room. She remembered a bright blue light coming through her window followed by a red light shining in her eyes. Now here she was lying on a flat firm, yet soft surface with a thin cover over her. The room was illuminated with a soft yellow glow from the ceiling. A panic feeling swept over her. She was cold and her stomach hurt.

A voice came into her mind, "I am Nog, your personal attendant. I sense that you are cold so will increase the mat temperature for you. Your stomach pain will gradually diminish." She looked to the left and saw a short gray alien with a big head and large black eyes. It had a small mouth and two breathing holes where a nose should be. Nog touched her and a calm feeling replaced the panic; she could now move her arms and legs.

"Now that you are awake, I will take you to be with the others." Nog gave her a one-piece light green garment like a poncho with a black symbol on the front and back. It had a flap across the chest area. She sat up and slipped it on over her head. Then she lay back down.

Nog pushed her into a larger room, also illuminated with a soft yellow glow, where she could hear women talking. After some time, she was able to sit up and look around. There were nine women sitting close together in a circle. They were all dressed in garments like hers. When they saw her, one of them said, "Oh no, they have taken another very young one." Sara managed to slip off the gurney and slowly walked over to them. She noticed that they were all the same ethnicity as she was. Some of them were probably early to mid 20's. Others were about her same age. She found a place to sit between two of them.

One of them said, "I am Nora, what is your name?"

"My name is Sara. What the heck is going on here?"

Nora said, "We have been taken for our ovum. Your stomach hurts because of the procedure they used to extract them from your uterus. Our ovum are taken and artificially inseminated with sperm from another alien race. Then they are put into an artificial uterus where they are nurtured. The babies are removed from the uterus device and two are given to each of their mothers for breast feeding. They look almost human, but have slightly larger heads, small ears and nose, and green eyes. They also grow faster and are much stronger than normal human babies. Your babies will be brought to you when they are able to breast feed."

"I was taken in early April. When were you taken?" Nora asked.

Sara said, "It was mid-March when they took me out of my bedroom in the middle of the night. I only remember a blue light coming in from the window and felt like someone was in my room. After that, I saw a red light shining in my eyes. I don't remember anything after that. The next thing I knew I was here in a small room."

Nora said, "We have all had a similar experience."

The young lady on her other side agreed. She asked, "Where were you at this time?"

Sara said, "I was in Hickory, North Carolina.

She replied, "I was in Denver, Colorado."

Nora said, "I was in Anchorage, Alaska."

Sara heard some activity from behind her. She turned to look and saw several small android grays, like Nog, wheeling in devices that looked like baby carriages. She also heard babies crying. Three of the women were each given two babies. They opened the flap across their chest and began to breast feed them. The babies looked just like Nora had described them. She felt a strange feeling of amazement, pity and disgust combined. The gray attendants waited until the feeding was over, picked up the babies, put them back in the carriages and wheeled them out of the room. They returned and motioned for the women to come with them. The women were led into a large round room with beds, tables, chairs and rest rooms, like a dormitory. It was also illuminated with a soft yellow light from the ceiling. The women began sitting at tables. Sara followed Nora and sat with her at a table. The gray attendants began bringing in bowls of food, placing them on the tables in front of them. Each of them was given the same food. It had a texture like thick mush and smelled like cooked cabbage. Eating utensils were located by each of their bowls, which looked like wooden tongue depressors.

Nora said, "It doesn't taste very good, but it seems to be nutritious as we are all very healthy. We are given two meals a day. This is the last one for today; after this, we have some leisure time before we go to bed. They don't have clocks, so we have no way to know the time, but it seems like a normal earth day. After we eat, we will be taken to a dormitory where we sleep. The next meal is after they turn the light back on and we are awakened. It is still like mush, but slightly different with a sweeter taste."

When the mealtime was over, the small grays came, picked up the bowls and cleaned the tables. The round wall turned into a garden scene like you would see on earth. The women got up from the tables and gathered in a seating area in the middle of the room. They were all eager to hear Sara's account of her abduction. When she finished telling them they each started talking in turn, sharing their own experiences. After some time, which seemed like a few hours, the ceiling illumination started to dim, the wall garden scene turned off and the room temperature began to cool. Soft music began that varied in pitch and volume. It had no discernible notes or timing; just wavering, soothing tones.

Nora said, "It is time to go to bed." She took Sara by the hand and led her to a bed beside hers, which was soft with a small pillow and cover. "I know that you must be very worried and stressed about this, but you will become accustomed to it after a while. We all had to go through this ordeal; we share our concerns among us and that helps a lot."

Sara laid there for a while thinking about all that had happened; however, she was so exhausted, she just went to sleep.

When she woke up, the room was lit, and the wall was again decorated with the garden scene. The other women were also beginning to wake up.

Nora said, "I see you are awake. I will stay with you and help you get used to the routine here. It is like a prison because we are all kept here and have no choice about how we are treated or what we do, but at least we are well cared for physically. I will introduce you to the others. We usually sit around and talk about our families or other things of interest until breakfast is served. There is also an exercise room that we can use. Come with me and I will show it to you."

They walked toward a doorway in the wall between two images of palm trees. As they approached, it automatically opened. Inside was another round room. This one was illuminated in the same way except the wall was decorated with a jungle scene and tropical animals. Nora showed her some exercise equipment like what would be found in a typical gymnasium. "We can come in here to work out any time we want. Some like to do yoga, others walk on the treadmills or around the room by the wall. The more athletic ones use the more sophisticated equipment to stay in shape." While they were talking, a light turned on over the door. Nora noticed it and said it was time for the first meal. They walked out and found the tables set with food for them.

Sara followed Nora to a table with two other women already seated at it. Nora introduced Sara to them. They eagerly shared their abduction experiences with Sara as they ate.

CHAPTER 4

THE NEGOTIATIONS

Early the next morning, #5 appeared while Joe's family were eating breakfast. He said, "We have the information from the Orion Collective about the layout of the Antarctic base and which parts are active. The AGC has analyzed it using heat signatures and they have a good idea of where Sara is being kept. If this is correct, she is alive and being well cared for. They believe that she is in an alien/human worker breeding program. It may be possible to negotiate her release. The AGC will send an ambassador for this purpose if that is what you want."

Joe said, "OH THANK GOD, that is very good news. Yes, of course, that is what we want! Please proceed! I will get you a current photograph of her. Let us know if there is anything else you need."

He went upstairs to Sara's bedroom and took down a recent photograph from the wall. He carried it downstairs, removed it from the frame and gave it to #5.

#5 said, "Yes, they will need this. I will get back to my AGC contact and ask him to start the negotiations. I will be back in touch with you when I have more information."

In the evening, two days later, #5 appeared and said, "My superior, #1, has been in contact with the AGC ambassador, who has been in touch with the Draco Antarctica Base Commander. They are willing to release Sara for a price. They want to exchange her for rare earth metals. The GFW has a stockpile of these so this may be possible; however, the quantity is high, and the metals wanted are very valuable, so that may be a problem. #1 has a meeting with a GFW director tomorrow to see it this can be done. I will get back to you when I have the information."

Joe said, "If there is anything I can do to help with this, just let me know."

#5 said, "I doubt that you will have enough resources of any kind to make a difference!" After saying this, he disappeared.

CHAPTER 6

THE PRICE

In the GFW director's office, #1 telepathically communicated with the director about the situation of Sara's abduction.

#1 reported, "The Terra human, Joe, was of great help to us with the pacification of Terra nations, which led to Terra's admission to the GFW. His daughter, Sara, was abducted by a crew from a Draco scout ship several days ago. We have found that she is in a human/alien breeding program at their Antarctic base. Joe and his family are very anxious about her and want her returned to them as soon as possible. The Ashtar Galactic Command has sent an ambassador to the Draco seeking a means of release for her. They have negotiated her return upon receiving a ransom payment."

The GFW director asked, "What is the ransom that they want?"

"They want rare earth metals that you have in your strategic stockpile," #1 replied.

"Which ones and how much of each?"

"They want 10 kilograms (KG) of neodymium and 3 KG each of dysprosium,   terbium and europium."

The director stated, "That is a very large demand! Does Joe have any assets that he is willing to put up toward this ransom?"

#1 answered, "He is a man of modest income who works as a manager in a furniture factory. He has a wife, named Ann, and one son, Dan, in addition to his daughter, Sara. He has a house and some other assets, but not enough to be of any consequence for this purpose."

"Tell me about his son."

#1 responded, "Dan is 18, a high school senior, and likes astronomy and computer science. He wants to be a space craft pilot."

"That is very interesting, the director commented. "We always have need for space craft pilots. Would he be willing to sign a ten-year employment contract with us?"

"Joe's family is very distraught about Sara's abduction; I believe Dan would be quite willing to sign the contract."

The director replied, "Tell them that we will put up the ransom if Dan is willing to come to work for us when he graduates from space pilot training."

"Thank you, sir. I am sure that Joe, his wife and Dan will agree to this arrangement."

The director said, "I want to see an agreement to this effect signed by Joe, Ann and Dan. Let me know when you have it, then I will arrange for removal of these rare earth metals from our strategic metals stockpile. I assume the AGC ambassador will be the one to make the trade? I will instruct the stockpile manager to turn these metals over to him at the appropriate time."

#1 telepathically communicated with #5 about the conversation he had with the GFW director and informed him how to proceed.

#5 immediately appeared at Joe's house. Joe had just gotten home from work. #5 told Joe of the agreement needed for the GFW to provide the ransom payment.

Joe discussed the plan with Ann and Dan that the GFW director had presented to #1. They talked briefly about it, agreed to write the contract and sign it. Joe wrote it, they all signed it and gave it to #5. He notified #1, informing him that it was signed. Immediately, #1 disappeared to give it to the GFW director.

#1 requested permission of the director to visit him. Upon receiving it, he appeared in the director's office. The director read and approved the contract. He communicated with the store house manager, informing him to prepare the precious metals needed and have them ready by tomorrow morning. Being aware of this telepathic communication, #1 thanked the GFW director for his generous help.

The next morning, as agreed, the AGC ambassador and two aids picked up the rare earth metals, which were in two metal boxes. The ambassador communicated with the Draco base commander and informed him that the ransom was in his possession. The Draco commander told him to bring them in the afternoon to the Antarctic base for the exchange.

At the designated time, the ambassador arrived at the base with the boxes. He was greeted by a Draco security guard at the base entrance. They took the boxes into the commander's office where he was waiting for them. The commander called for a metals specialist to come to his office. The specialist opened the boxes and checked the contents for purity and weight. He informed the commander that the metals and weights were according to the agreement. The commander then informed the breeding program manager to have Sara removed from the program and brought to his office.

Sara had just finished the second meal and was headed for the exercise room with Nora when Nog came up to her. Nog requested she come with him. Nora was surprised as something like this had never happened before. Sara followed Nog out of the room. Nog took her to the commander's office. There she was greeted by the AGC ambassador. He looked at the photograph of Sara, Joe had provided, to verify that she was the right person. He then told Sara she would be released and taken home.

Sara said, "OH, THANK YOU GOD!" and began sobbing with relief at the news. The commander instructed Nog to take her to a waiting room where she would stay until the ambassador could arrange her transportation.

The AGC ambassador communicated with #5 and informed him that Sara had been released and was waiting for transportation to take her home. He also informed him that his security clearance had been granted and that he should come to the Antarctic base commander's office where he could pick her up.

#5 appeared at Joe's house where they had just finished eating breakfast. He told Joe and the others that the ransom had been paid, and that Sara was free to come home.

Joe said, "We have been praying for her release! God has answered our prayers." He went over to Ann and Dan and told them the good news. They all started sobbing and praising God for His loving care for them.

#5 said, "I have been given permission to go to the Draco Antarctic base commander's office to pick her up." After saying this, he disappeared.

#5 appeared in a transparent sphere at the commander's office as instructed. He stepped out of the sphere and greeted the commander.

The Draco commander greeted him back and told the security guard to bring Sara to his office. When Sara came in, #5 explained to her who he was, that he had previously worked with her father, and that he was here to take her back home. She remembered her father talking about how he had worked with #5 to bring Terra into the GFW.

Sara experienced mixed emotions. She was overjoyed at the thought of going home and at the same time she was amazed at the appearance of #5 and his offer to take her home.

#5 took her by the hand and said that the transparent sphere was her transportation. He then stepped into the sphere with her. As soon as they were inside, the sphere disappeared from the Draco commander's office.

They immediately appeared in the front room of Joe's home. The sphere disappeared and left them standing there.

Sara called out: "I am home." Hearing her voice, Joe, Ann and Dan rushed into the front room to greet her.

Joe said, "Thank God you are home safe." They all hugged each other and began sobbing with joy. After a few minutes, Joe turned to #5 and thanked him profusely for what he had done.

#5 said he was thankful that she was home, and glad that he could be of service.

"Sara will probably have trauma from her abduction. You should take her to HHH for Post Traumatic Stress Disorder (PTSD) healing." Saying that, #5 disappeared.

CHAPTER 7

SARA'S BABIES

1 7 years later, Joe is retired from his job at the furniture factory. He has a hobby of repairing robots in his garage.

Ann writes software programs to upgrade the robots. They have 2 personal robots that do the house and yard work.

Dan has graduated from the Space Craft Academy and is in pilot training at the GFW space craft port in Florida.

Sara is a doctor working with patients at the local hospital. She examines patients and decides which form and duration of medbed treatment would be best for them. Patient healing time in the medbed can be from a few hours to several weeks.

Cars are now called Personal Transportation Vehicles (PTV) that use artificial intelligence (AI) controls. They are like a cab without a cab driver. You get in one, tell it where you want to go, and it takes you there without any actions by the occupant. They can fly if you want to go some distance. They fly at constant speed in designated elevated lanes for North, South, East and West. The lanes are separated by 20 meters in all directions and PTV's cannot change lanes once they are in motion. They have automatic separation controls, which keep them at a minimum of 10 meters from each other. If the PTV senses any defect, it automatically goes to the nearest repair garage.

It is possible to travel to other planets in our solar system as well as those in other solar systems by use of passenger space craft. Large cities are below the surface of Mars, Venus, Jupiter and Saturn.

One Sunday after church, Joe, Ann and Sara were relaxing in the living room when the doorbell rang. Joe went to answer the door. When he opened it there were 2 tall, handsome very well-built young men standing there.

Joe said, "How can I help you?"

One of them said, "We came to see Sara. Is she home?"

Joe said, "Yes, what do you want to see her about?"

One of them said, "I am SA23, and he is SA24. Sara is our mother. We wanted to get acquainted with her. We checked the records from the Draco breeding program at Antarctica and obtained the information about her from them."

After standing there at the door in surprised amazement, Joe invited them into the house. When they walked into the living room where Ann and Sara were, they both looked up at the young men with puzzled looks on their faces.

Joe said, "This is SA23, and he is SA24. They are Sara's children from the alien breeding program." Ann and Sara's look of puzzlement changed to one of amazement.

Sara said, "You mean that I am their mother?"

Joe said, "Apparently that is so."

Ann said, "Then I am their grandmother, and you are their grandfather."

Joe said, "Looks that way. Our family just got bigger."

Ann invited them to sit down and said, "Tell us about yourselves, where are you living and what do you do."

SA23 said, "We live and work at the GFW cargo terminal in Florida. We load and unload cargo space craft arriving and departing. We use robots to do most of the work, but there are some packages that require movement by hand. We can each lift 125 KG (about 275 pounds) but when we get older and stronger we will be able to lift twice that amount."

Ann asked, "How did you get away from the Draco?"

SA24 replied, "Several months after Sara was released, the GFW pressured the base commander into freeing the other mothers. They were returned to their families. Those of us who were still in the artificial wombs were allowed to mature. When we were old enough, the GFW hired us to work for them at the space cargo terminal."

Sara asked, "Are there any others like you from my ovum?"

SA24 replied, "The records showed that there were 24 total viable zygotes but when you were removed from the program, we were the only 2 that were given to another mother for breast feeding and further nurturing. The other 22 were terminated."

Sara asked, "Do you know who your father is?

SA24 replied, "We do not know his name, but we do know he was a Selosian. That is the reason we have green eyes and blond hair."

Ann asked if they would like to stay for dinner.

SA23 answered, "We would like to, but we need to get back to the terminal. Our shift starts in one hour."

Ann said, "Perhaps you could come some other time."

SA23 said, "Yes, we would like to. We will contact you when we are available."

They exchanged contact information.

Ann said, "That will be good. We can have a nice conversation and get better acquainted. What do you like to eat?"

SA23 said, "We like mostly vegetables, but eat some fish and other sea food."

Ann said, "That would be lovely. I will be happy to prepare a meal that we can all enjoy."

SA23 and SA24 stood up to leave. Joe went over to them and shook hands. He said, I will walk you out." Sara and Ann joined them as they walked to the door.

Ann said, "This has been a pleasant surprise, and we look forward to seeing you again."

The two brothers walked to their PTV parked in the driveway. They waved goodbye as they got in. The PTV backed out of the driveway, onto the street and drove away.

CHAPTER 8

SUMMARY

The next week, SA23 and SA24 arranged with Joe, Ann and Sara to have dinner. Ann prepared fish, vegetables and a delicious dessert.

During the meal, Joe told them about their son Dan was in training at the GFW space port.

SA23 said, We would like to find him and introduce ourselves."

Joe said, "I am sure he would appreciate that." Joe gave them Dan's contact information.

When the evening was over, Ann thought about her experience meeting her grandchildren for the first time. She remembered how Joe had assisted the aliens to bring harmony to earth and how aliens, in turn, had brought an extended family into her life through Sara's abduction. From being involved with aliens in the past to now having them as part of her family, she felt like her life had become more meaningful.

www.ingramcontent.com/pod-product-compliance
Lightning Source LLC
Chambersburg PA
CBHW020653010826
48969CB00012B/862